ATTACK OF THE MUTANT LUNCH LADY

Librarian Reviewer
Katharine Kan
Graphic novel reviewer and Library Consultant, Panama City, FL
MLS in Library and Information Studies, University of Hawaii at
Manoa, HI

Reading Consultant
Elizabeth Stedem
Educator/Consultant, Colorado Springs, CO
MA in Elementary Education, University of Denver, CO

▼▼ STONE ARCH BOOKS
MINNEAPOLIS   SAN DIEGO

Graphic Sparks are published by Stone Arch Books
151 Good Counsel Drive, P.O. Box 669
Mankato, Minnesota 56002
www.stonearchbooks.com

Library of Congress Cataloging-in-Publication Data
Nickel, Scott.
    Attack of the Mutant Lunch Lady: A Buzz Beaker Brainstorm / by Scott Nickel;
illustrated by Andy J Smith.
    p. cm. — (Graphic Sparks—A Buzz Beaker Brainstorm)
    ISBN 978-1-4342-0451-6 (library binding)
    ISBN 978-1-4342-0501-8 (paperback)
    1. Graphic novels. I. Smith, Andy J., 1975– II. Title.
PN6727.N544A88 2008
741.5'973—dc22   2007031250

Summary: Brainy Buzz Beaker thought nothing could be grosser than cafeteria food.
That's before the school's lunch lady turned into a mutant blob of mystery meat. Now,
Buzz and his best friend, Larry, must discover a way to stop the Cafeteria Creature.

Art Director: Heather Kindseth
Graphic Designer: Brann Garvey

1 2 3 4 5 6 13 12 11 10 09 08

9

29

33

ABOUT THE AUTHOR

Born in 1962 in Denver, Colorado, Scott Nickel works by day at Paws, Inc., Jim Davis's famous Garfield studio, and he freelances by night. Burning the midnight oil, Scott has created hundreds of humorous greeting cards and written several children's books, short fiction for *Boys' Life* magazine, comic strips, and lots of really funny knock-knock jokes. He was raised in southern California, but in 1995 Scott moved to Indiana, where he currently lives with his wife, two sons, six cats, and several sea monkeys.

ABOUT THE ILLUSTRATOR

From a young age, Andy Smith knew he wanted to be an illustrator (if he couldn't be a space adventurer, superhero, or ghost hunter). After graduating from college in 1998, he began working at a handful of New York City animation studios on shows like *Courage the Cowardly Dog* and *Sheep in the Big City,* while also working in freelance illustration. Andy has since left New York City for Rochester, NY where he teaches high school art and illustration at the Rochester Institute of Technology.

GLOSSARY

brew (BROO)—a boiling, bubbling, steaming mixture of two or more ingredients

cafeteria (kaf-uh-TEER-ee-uh)—the place where students are served food, or some type of mystery meat

chemical reaction (KEM-uh-kuhl ree-AK-shuhn)—the often dangerous response that happens when two chemicals mix

grammar (GRAM-ur)—the correct way to speak and write. This sentence ain't got no proper grammar.

hairpiece (HAYR-peess)—a wig or section of fake hair used to cover a bald spot

mystery meat (MISS-tur-ee MEET)—a mix of many unknown meats into a single dish. Hot dogs, Spam, and bologna are mystery meats (and they're not so bad, are they?).

perfume (PUR-fyoom)—a scented liquid that people spray onto their skin

permanent (PUR-muh-nuhnt)—lasting for a long, long time. Something on your **permanent** record at school will be there FOREVER!

toxic (TOK-sik)—harmful to your health

MORE ABOUT YOUR LUNCH

Some people say, "You are what you eat." Of course, they don't mean that you'll actually mutate into a mystery meat monster! But if you eat healthy foods, your body will be healthy too. Along with daily exercise, the MyPyramid plan can help you choose the right foods to keep your body at its best.

Each colored section of the MyPyramid plan represents an important food group.

Orange: Grains

The grain group includes rice, pastas, bread, tortillas, cereal, and much more. Try for whole grains if you can. They'll give you more long-lasting energy.

Green: Vegetables

Eat a variety of vegetables every day. It shouldn't be tough. There are more than 5,000 varieties of potatoes alone!

Red: Fruits

Fresh, frozen, canned, or dried, there are many ways to eat this group. Filling up on fruit should be a breeze.

Yellow: Oils

Oils come from many sources, including butter, shortening, nuts, and fish. But there's a reason this colored section is only a sliver. Only a little oil should be eaten every day.

Blue: Milk

The milk group is more than the white stuff you pour on top of cereal. This group includes cheese, yogurt, pudding, and even ice cream!

Purple: Meat and Beans

Both meat and beans have protein, which helps your body build strong muscles.

DISCUSSION QUESTIONS

1. Do you think author Scott Nickel wanted the Cafeteria Creature to be funny, scary, or a little bit of both? Explain your answer.

2. What's your favorite thing to eat for lunch? Would you rather eat a cafeteria meal or bring food from home?

3. In this story, illustrator Andy Smith drew the lunch lady three different ways. Look back at the illustrations and describe how this character changed from the beginning, middle, and the end. Which version do you like the best and why?

WRITING PROMPTS

1. Write a story about your ultimate dream lunch. If you could invite any three people in the world to join you, who would they be? What would you talk about? What would you eat for your lunch?

2. In this story, Buzz Beaker had a pretty weird day at school. Describe the weirdest, wildest, or wackiest day you've ever had at school.

3. Buzz's friend, Larry, is a really kooky kid. But in the story, we don't learn a lot about his life outside school. Write your own story about Larry's family, friends, pets, and hobbies.